A Koala Grows Up

By Rita Golden Gelman
Illustrated by Gioia Fiammenghi

Scholastic Inc.
New York Toronto London Auckland Sydney

For my mother and father
with love and thanks.
R.G.G.

ISBN 0-590-41869-6

12 11 10 9 8 7 6 5 4 3 2 1 2 3 4 5/9

Printed in the U.S.A. 08

Koalas live along the eastern coast of Australia.
They grow to be 25 to 35 inches tall.
They usually weigh from 15 to 30 pounds.
Some have gray fur, some have brown fur,
and some have fur that is yellowish-brown.

Sometimes we call them "koala bears,"
but they are not bears.
Koalas are marsupials.
That means they live inside their mothers' pouches
when they are babies.
They live with their mothers until they are about
two years old.
Then they go off on their own.

This is the story of one little koala.

It was night in the forest.
An owl was hooting.
A wombat was scratching in the dirt,
looking for roots to eat.
Three glider possums were playing
follow-the-leader.

Suddenly a strange, harsh screech
sounded through the air.
The cry came again and again.
It was a male koala, calling for a mate.

A small female koala heard the calls.
She ran down her tree to the tree of the male.
That night they mated.

A month later, the female koala
felt something move inside her.
Soon her cub was born.

The pink, shiny cub was tiny —
about the size of a bee.
He couldn't see or hear.
His face did not even look like a face.
It had three little holes in it —
two for nostrils and one for his mouth.

The cub dug his sharp, tiny claws
into his mother's fur.
He pulled himself toward her pouch.

At last he reached the pouch
and crawled inside.
He began to drink his mother's milk.

For months the koala cub snuggled
inside the pouch.
He kept drinking . . . and growing.

At six months the cub was
seven inches long.
He had four strong legs.
He had soft, brown fur.
He could see and he could hear.

He was ready to come out
of the pouch.

Wild koalas live in eucalyptus trees
in the forests of Australia.
Eucalyptus trees are also called gum trees.
The cub and his mother lived in
their own red gum tree.

All day long, the two koalas slept there.
At night, the cub and his mother woke up.
The cub crawled onto his mother's chest.
He sniffed the sweet smell of the red gum tree.

His mother climbed from branch to branch.
She pulled off leaves and ate them.
Koalas have two thumbs on each hand
to help them pull off leaves.

The baby koala watched carefully.
Then he tried to pull a leaf off, too.

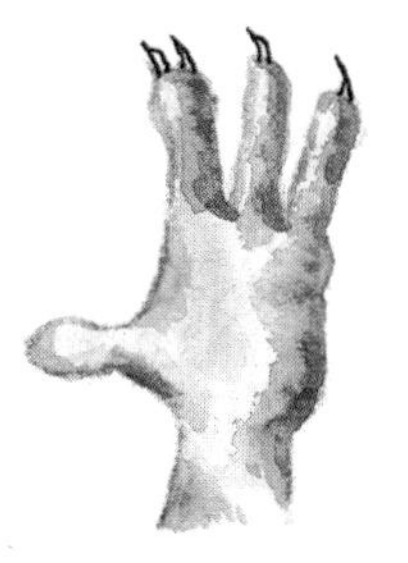

When he was about eight months old,
he climbed onto his mother's back
for the first time.
The koala was growing up.

One evening
the cub spotted a bird on a branch.
He wanted to play.

Out he went to the end of the branch.
But the branch was too thin.
It wobbled wildly!
The koala's foot slipped.
Suddenly he was hanging upside down.
He let out a shriek.

Using his claws, he slowly
pulled himself back to the trunk.
He ran to his mother. At last he was safe.

Summer came. The days were long and hot.
There was no rain.
The grass turned brown.

Finally the river dried up.
Many animals left the forest to find water.

The koalas did not have to worry about water.
They got all the water they needed
from eucalyptus leaves.
The word *koala* means "does not drink."

One day, there was a strange smell.
Far away, the cub saw black clouds.

That night, fire flashed in the darkness.
Smoke surrounded the koala's tree.
Many animals were running from the fire.
But the young koala and his mother
stayed in their tree.
They climbed as high as they could go.

Closer and closer came the fire.
The hot smoke made the koalas
cough and cry as the fire closed in
on their tree.

Suddenly the wind changed direction.
The fire raced off toward the riverbed.
The young koala and his mother were safe.
But their tree had been badly burned.
Almost all the leaves were gone.

So the mother koala set off with her cub
to find a new red gum tree.

Night after night the koalas kept going.
During the day, they slept in a tree.
They ate nothing.
They were looking for red gum leaves.

Then one night, the koalas smelled
something good —
the oil from a red gum tree!

The koalas followed the smell.

Soon they came to a river.
On the other side of the river
was a forest of red gum trees.
The mother swam across with her cub
on her back.

The koalas climbed the trunk
of a big red gum tree
and began to eat . . . and eat . . . and eat.

The cub was growing.
Some nights he practiced jumping.
He climbed above his mother
and pounced on her back.
His mother didn't mind.
She just kept eating.

As the cub grew, he explored farther and farther
away from his mother.
Sometimes he jumped from one tree to another.
But each morning he came back
to sleep on his mother's back.

One night, the cub was eating leaves
at the very top of the tree.
Suddenly an owl swooped down,
ready to snatch the little koala.

The cub looked up just in time.
He spread his legs and slid down the tree
to the ground.

By the time the cub was two years old,
he was bigger than his mother.
Now she wouldn't let him climb
on her back.
The cub found his own branch to sleep on.

Soon the cub wanted his own tree.
He climbed down
from his mother's tree.
He began walking.

When the sun came up,
the cub was curled up in his own tree,
far away from his mother.

Then one night, when the moon was full
and the wombats were digging,
and the owls were hooting,
and the other koalas were eating leaves,
the young koala stood near the top of his tree.
Suddenly he let out a loud, harsh shriek.
Again and again, his cry pierced the air.
He was calling for a mate.

And a female koala heard the calls
and walked toward his tree. . . .